A SECRET DIARY OF
THE FIRST
WORLD WAR

To all the boys who never came home. – G.A.

For Grandpa Gate. Too young to fight in a war,
too old to escape it. He taught me a lot. – D.G.

Kelpies is an imprint of Floris Books
First published in 2018 by Floris Books

The publisher acknowledges subsidy from
Creative Scotland towards the publication
of this volume

MIX
Paper from
responsible sources
FSC® C117931
FSC
www.fsc.org

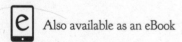

Also available as an eBook

British Library CIP data available
ISBN 978-178250-527-3
Printed & bound by MBM Print SCS Ltd, Glasgow

FACT-TASTIC STORIES FROM SCOTLAND'S HISTORY

A SECRET DIARY OF THE FIRST WORLD WAR

WRITTEN BY GILL ARBUTHNOTT

ILLUSTRATED BY DARREN GATE

Young Kelpies

CONTENTS

THE OUTBREAK OF WAR

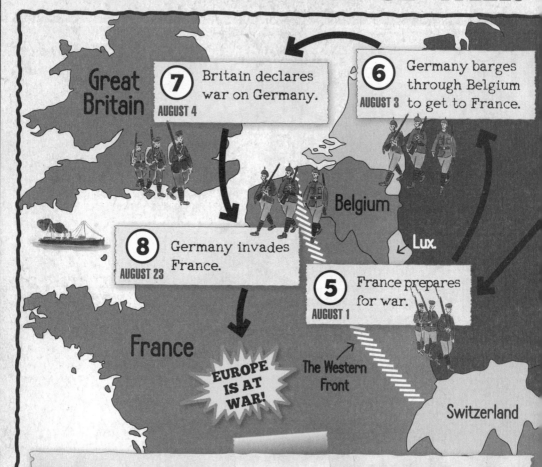

Great Britain

7 **AUGUST 4** Britain declares war on Germany.

6 **AUGUST 3** Germany barges through Belgium to get to France.

8 **AUGUST 23** Germany invades France.

Belgium

Lux.

5 **AUGUST 1** France prepares for war.

France

EUROPE IS AT WAR!

The Western Front

Switzerland

In 1914 Europe was ruled by large empires. Some countries were friends, others were old enemies. Some wanted to be free from their bossy rulers, others were hungry for more land and power. The Bosnian **Black Hand** terrorists wanted freedom from the Austro-Hungarian Empire so they could unite with their friends in Serbia. On 28th June they killed the heir to the Empire's throne, Archduke Franz Ferdinand, which made the rulers of lots of countries very angry. They divided into two opposing sides, the Allies and the Central Powers.

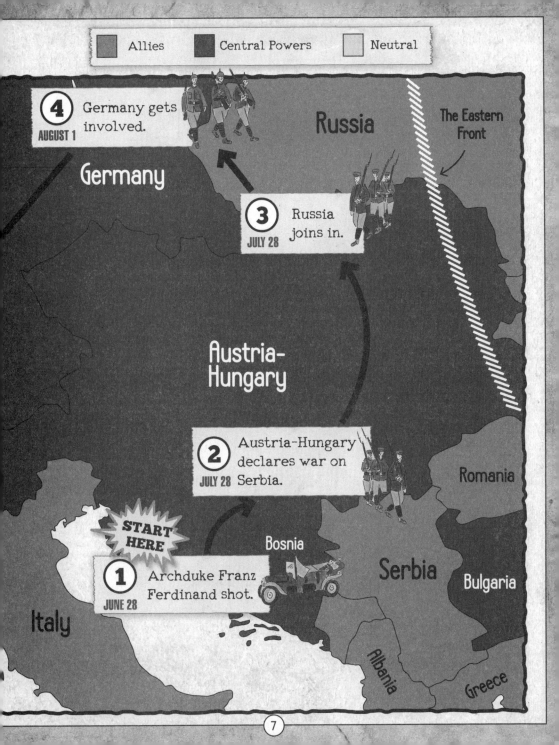

Allies   Central Powers   Neutral

4 Germany gets involved.
AUGUST 1

Russia

The Eastern Front

Germany

3 Russia joins in.
JULY 28

Austria-Hungary

2 Austria-Hungary declares war on Serbia.
JULY 28

START HERE

Bosnia

Serbia

Romania

1 Archduke Franz Ferdinand shot.
JUNE 28

Italy

Albania

Bulgaria

Greece

DALKEITH, SCOTLAND, 4TH AUGUST 1914

I'm going to war. I can hardly believe it. Yesterday I was delivering rolls and newspapers as usual, and today I've been called up to go to France and fight with my army battalion, the Royal Scots.

I suppose I should write a bit about myself, in case anyone else ever reads this. My name is James Marchbank, I'm fourteen and I'm from Dalkeith, near Edinburgh in Scotland. I left school in June and since then I've been working as a delivery boy. My father's a coal miner and Mother's always busy looking after us seven children. Margaret's oldest, then William, then me, then the four wee ones.

While I was still at school I joined the army part-time in one of the Royal Scots territorial battalions as a bugler and drummer – I've been playing the bugle since I first joined the Boy Scouts. My army pay was a bit of extra money for the family, and I've always fancied being a soldier. I really enjoyed training at the weekends, but now I've been called up to the army full time, to go to France and fight Jerry (that's what folk are calling the Germans now). I never saw that coming.

My bugle

Mother looked worried when my call-up papers arrived today, but she didn't say much, just set to finding a bag for my bits and pieces and putting some food together for me. Father took a pull on his pipe, like he always does when he's thinking hard, and said, "Don't get too excited, lad. You've to finish training before you get anywhere near France. Likely it'll all be over before you get the chance to join in."

I hope he's wrong – I'd choose adventures in France over trudging the streets with deliveries any day. Deep down I'm a bit worried about the fighting, of course, but I'm not going to think about that just now.

ARMY PAY

At the start of the First World War a private in the Territorial Forces was paid 1 shilling (5 pence) per day. Boys like James only got half pay – 2½ pence! This was worth about the same as £2.75 today.

NETTLES

The Germans used nettles to make army shirts. It took 40 kg of nettles to make fabric for 1 shirt. They were probably a bit itchy, but they didn't sting once they'd been processed.

WHO JOINED THE ARMY AND WHY?

ENLIST IN THE ARMY!

August 1914

In 1914, 14-year-old James was called up with the rest of his battalion to fight because he had already joined up, or enlisted. Soon after the war started, regulations changed so that only men of 18 and over could enlist in the army, and they had to be 19 to fight overseas.

I've decided to enlist and go to France to fight. I'm fed up with my dull life here — it's just work and home and work again, and never enough money to do anything for fun. Me and my pals want an adventure together, and this is our best chance. We're not old enough, but I've heard that if you say you're nineteen the army takes you, even if they don't believe you, so we're all going to enlist tomorrow.

— Donald, age 17

We had been brought up to believe that Britain was the best country in the world and we wanted to defend her.

Private George Morgan, 16th Battalion, West Yorkshire Regiment

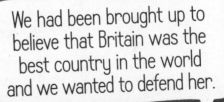

BRITAIN

"WANTS" **YOU**

JOIN YOUR COUNTRY'S ARMY!

GOD SAVE THE KING

CONSCRIPTION
May 1916

All able-bodied men aged between 18 and 41 now had to join the armed forces, except those whose work was needed at home:

- miners
- ship builders
- train drivers
- doctors
- clergymen
- teachers
- steelworkers

Women could enlist as cooks, drivers and office workers, but not as soldiers.

11TH DECEMBER 1918

THE SPORTING BATTALION

The sportsmen of Edinburgh were swift to answer the call to defend their country on the outbreak of war, many enlisting in the 16th Royal Scots – McCrae's Battalion. Notably, sixteen players from Heart of Midlothian football team fought on the Western Front with the 16th. Seven lost their lives in the conflict, and many of the others were wounded, some so badly that their footballing careers are over. We must never forget the sacrifices made by these brave young men.

HADDINGTON, SCOTLAND, 14TH SEPTEMBER 1914

I need bigger boots. My feet must have grown since I got to the training camp here in East Lothian. It's a wonder they're not worn away to stumps, the amount of marching we do – 20 miles some days. You should see my blisters.

We've been learning how to shoot and Sergeant Grieves says I'm a good shot. I'm pleased about that – at least I'll be useful when I get to the Western Front. And we've been practising with bayonets – it's all right shoving one into a sack of straw with a face painted on it, but I can't  imagine doing it to a living man. I dreamed last night that some huge German was doing it to me, and I woke myself up shouting at him.

There are hundreds of men here. Some of them have been part-time soldiers in the Territorial Forces like us. We already know what we're doing, more or less. But the men who've come straight from civvy street haven't got a clue. They don't even have uniforms yet, and they look funny marching, all dressed differently. A lot of them aren't very fit, puffing and blowing at the first wee bit hill, and some of them don't have boots, just shoes, which are falling apart after so much marching over rough ground. The officers will have a job turning this lot into soldiers who'll be able to take on the Germans.

It's my job to wake everyone in the morning with my bugle. I'm the most unpopular lad in camp for a couple of minutes then, but otherwise we all get on well enough. A lot of the men in the battalion are from Dalkeith: Charlie Smith, Tommy Turnbull, Richard Peacock (not that I see much of him now they've made him up to sergeant). They know my family and think it's very funny that I'm here but my brother

William isn't. He's too young to enlist in the army, even though he's two years older than me! That's a puzzle, right enough. William's furious, and says he's going to lie about his age so he can join up. Felix McNamara from the Post Office is here too. He's a sergeant. He said, "Keep close to me when we get to the Front, lad. I'll look after you."

This is Felix

GET KNITTING

By November 1914, the army needed 300,000 pairs of socks. Almost every woman in Britain was knitting as fast as possible!

Father was wrong about the fighting being over before we get there. We've just been told we'll be at the Front by November. I wonder if I'll still be there at Christmas or if we'll have beaten Jerry by then?

THE ENGLISH CHANNEL, 4TH NOVEMBER 1914

We were on a train for nearly a day to get to Southampton – so crammed in we were glad to get off and march through town to the docks. There were people everywhere, cheering us on. It made us feel like heroes even though we haven't done anything yet.

We got our own rifles just before they packed us onto smelly old cattle boats. We're almost across the Channel now, and it's been horrible – chop and slap, up and down through the waves, and the stink of bullocks. I puked most of the way.

It's gone very quiet on the boat. We've just been told there's a U-boat out there somewhere. I've heard they carry torpedoes that could sink any ship. Everyone's keeping watch. Got to go.

GERMAN U-BOAT
(UNTERSEEBOOT)

Depth charges could be used
to destroy them underwater

Crew of 35 men

Diameter: 3.7 m

← 47 m long →

Batteries, which released
poisonous gas if they got wet

German U-boats didn't take part
in battles, but were used to sink
Allied ships transporting supplies
and soldiers. They sank around
2600 ships during the war.

Germany had 29 U-boats at the
start of the First World War and
built 360 more during the war.
202 of them were destroyed,
killing over 5000 men.

U-boats could spend up to 5 days on
patrol, but only had enough air to
stay underwater for 3 days, so they
often had to come to the surface,
where they were easy targets.

THE BATTLE OF
MAY ISLAND

The British navy also had some
submarines. In 1917 about 40
British vessels, including 9
submarines, left Rosyth on the
Firth of Forth to head to Orkney.
But due to foggy weather
and poor communications two
submarines crashed into each
other near the Isle of May in the
Forth and sank, killing 104 people.

KITTED OUT

Greatcoat

Webbing harness

Bayonet

Rifle

Grenades

Extra socks

Rations for two days

Blanket

150 rounds of ammunition

Gloves

Groundsheet/ rain cape

Mess tin

Water bottle

Entrenching tool

Puttees: cloth leg wraps worn over trousers for support and protection.

Cutlery and shaving kit

Field dressing

FIRST AID KIT

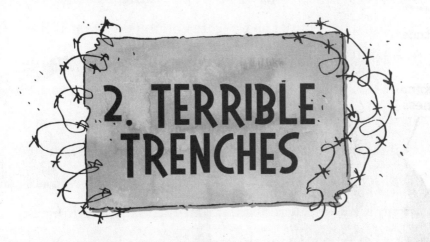

2. TERRIBLE TRENCHES

BOIS GRENIER, NORTHERN FRANCE, 15TH NOVEMBER 1914

We're in the trenches, near the Belgian border. We got the train from Le Havre, then marched and marched through France until I thought my feet would drop off. The first trenches we reached weren't much more than holes in the mud a man could hide in, but nearer the front line they're much deeper, and I can only see out of them if I stand up on the firestep. Not that I'm daft enough to put my head above the parapet after what happened to Sergeant Grieve – he was killed by a sniper as we were coming up towards the front-line trenches. He'd just finished saying, "Keep your heads down, lads, the trench isn't deep enough here and there's still enough light for snipers!" And then he fell. I thought he'd just tripped, but he didn't get up again. I've never seen a dead body before. There was just a wee hole in the middle of his forehead. It hardly looked anything, but he's gone. It was so quick. I can't believe a life can end just like a candle being blown out.

We'd been staying in a farmhouse near the trenches until it was shelled a few hours ago. Nobody had been expecting it and there were men running and officers shouting orders and complete chaos for a few minutes when the terrible booming noise started. The buildings near the house were destroyed – just piles of rubble left. Two horses killed, but no men, thank goodness – the shells missed the main house. I panicked and ran outside as soon as I heard the first explosion, and then ran back in to get my bugle. What was I thinking? If a shell had hit the farmhouse I would have been blown to pieces. I'll try to keep my head next time and not do anything that stupid again.

BOIS GRENIER, 10TH DECEMBER 1914

The weather's been too bad for big battles – who knew weather could be in charge of a war?

We're all digging in for the winter, the Germans too; making sure the trenches are deep and well shored-up with wood and sandbags, plenty of barbed wire in front of them and good positions for our snipers. Now that there's a proper trench system we have to sleep in them more often – no more comfy farmhouses! I spend a lot of time with the mining lads, who know how to dig trenches without them collapsing.

TRENCH FOOT

Soldiers often spent days with their feet in water, which could lead to a very painful condition called trench foot, then gangrene and even amputation. To prevent trench foot, soldiers were meant to rub whale oil into each other's feet, but it was very smelly.

IN THE TRENCHES
TRENCH STRUCTURE

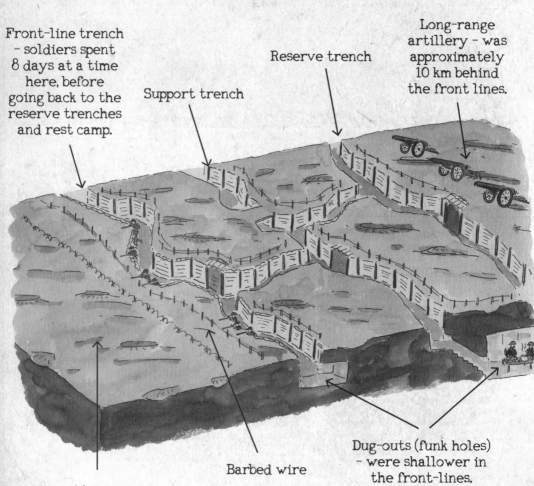

Front-line trench - soldiers spent 8 days at a time here, before going back to the reserve trenches and rest camp.

Support trench

Reserve trench

Long-range artillery - was approximately 10 km behind the front lines.

No man's land - the stretch of land between enemy trenches was roughly 25-300 m apart.

Barbed wire

Dug-outs (funk holes) - were shallower in the front-lines.

A FRONT-LINE TRENCH

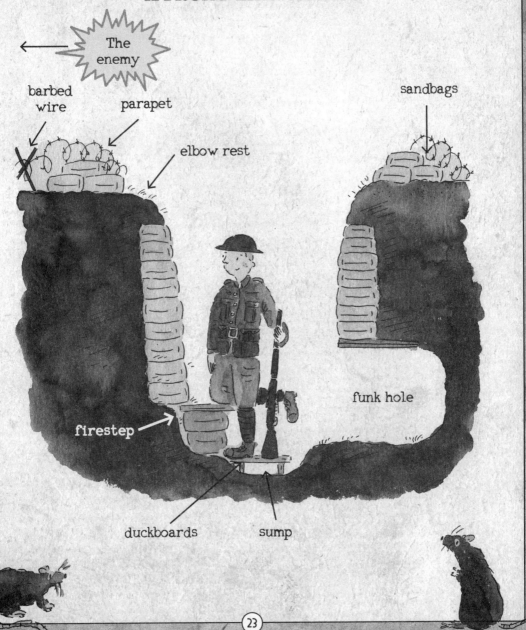

The enemy

barbed wire

parapet

elbow rest

sandbags

firestep

duckboards

sump

funk hole

Sometimes I get put on bringing rations up from the field kitchens behind the reserve trenches. I thought it would be a safe job, but Jerry often takes shots at us as we struggle along with the food, or sends over a shell or two. There's no bugle playing to be done here on the front line, although I play when we march from place to place.

Hot food's a real treat, but it's usually cold by the time we get it back from the kitchens. Everyone shovels it down, though, however bad it is. Sometimes we can cook ourselves a bit of bacon for breakfast, but other times it's just bread and jam, and the same for tea, or maybe bread and cheese. Some days it's nothing at all. We've got iron rations in our kits, with biscuits and tinned stew, (I wonder why they're called iron rations – maybe because the biscuits in them are so hard?) but we're not allowed to eat them without permission. They're supposed to be kept in case we're under fire and can't

RATION BISCUITS

So hard they were almost inedible, men often used ration biscuits as fuel to boil water in 'dixies', or even carved them into things like picture frames to send home.

get anything else. I've never been this hungry or cold before. I'd give anything for a plate of Mother's mince and tatties in front of the kitchen fire. I dream about home. But then I wake up and I'm still here.

Here's what we do most days:

DAWN: we 'stand to' – on the alert, rifles ready – for an hour in case of attack. It's only half-light then, and often misty, so we're never sure what might be going on in no man's land. If nothing happens we get some time to snatch a nap, unless we're on sentry duty – then breakfast.

DAYTIME: we 'clean' our trenches. That's a laugh – how are you meant to keep a hole in the ground clean? Especially with the buckets we have to use as toilets. But we clear up as best we can to try and keep the rats away. Then we clean our rifles and they're inspected. We bring up supplies from behind the lines, work in the trenches building firesteps or digging funkholes, fill sandbags with earth and use them to build up the edge of the trench. That's OK if the weather's been dry, but just you try digging a hole in mud! Sometimes we have a rat hunt to pass the time, or write letters home, or diaries like this one, and we sleep whenever we get the chance.

EVENING: if it's still quiet, dinner gets sent up from the field kitchens, then we work until near dusk, then stand to again.

NIGHT: once it's dark, we're out of the trenches to empty the toilet buckets, repair wire, or dig new trenches out into no man's land.

If I'm honest, it's boring when it's not frightening. So far, it's not the adventure I'd imagined. And it won't be over by Christmas.

BOIS GRENIER, 24TH DECEMBER 1914

Christmas Eve in the front-line trenches is pretty miserable.

I shouldn't complain though – if I'd been forward on the 18th

I might be dead by now. There was a German attack and we

lost a lot of men. I knew a couple of them – Rob Muir and

Richard Peacock. I keep imagining their families getting the

telegram. I can't believe I'll never see them again.

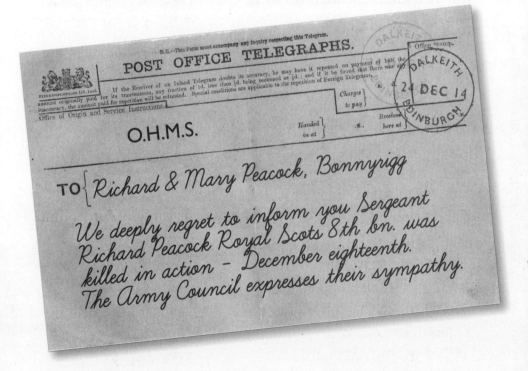

POST OFFICE TELEGRAPHS.

N.B.—This Form must accompany any Inquiry respecting this Telegram.

If the Receiver of an Inland Telegram doubts its accuracy, he may have it repeated on payment of half the amount originally paid for its transmission, any fraction of 1d. less than ½d. being reckoned as ½d.; and if it be found that there was any inaccuracy, the amount paid for repetition will be refunded. Special conditions are applicable to the repetition of Foreign Telegrams.

Office of Origin and Service Instructions.

Office Stamp.

DALKEITH EDINBURGH 24 DEC 14

Charges to pay

O.H.M.S.

Handed in at

M.

Received here at

TO { Richard & Mary Peacock, Bonnyrigg

We deeply regret to inform you Sergeant Richard Peacock Royal Scots 8th bn. was killed in action – December eighteenth. The Army Council expresses their sympathy.

> We had a tremendous number of frostbite cases at the beginning of 1917... Some of their toes dropped off with it.

Nurse Kathleen Yardwood

I'm up to my knees in water today, it's rained so much. I don't think I'll ever be dry or warm again, and I itch everywhere from louse bites. Ugh! They're horrible things and everyone has them. Every so often a rat swims past and I try to skewer it with my bayonet, just for something to do.

Too cold to write any more.

LICE

Almost everyone in the trenches had body lice, which are about twice the size of head lice. Apart from itching, their bites could cause trench fever, which made soldiers too ill to fight. The lice laid eggs in the seams of uniforms, which made them very hard to remove. Soldiers sometimes burned them out with candles, but had to take care not to set their clothes on fire!

RATS

Rats were a constant problem in the trenches. They would feed on scraps of food and on dead bodies. Sometimes they would bite sleeping soldiers. Many soldiers wrote about how huge they were.

BOIS GRENIER, 25TH DECEMBER 1914

Merry Christmas! Well, maybe not. It stopped raining last night, and was so cold the water started to freeze. No shooting from either side this morning, just a strange silence. We're only about 50 yards from the German trenches here, and as it got light they started to sing. After a bit we realised they were singing 'Silent Night' in German.

Johnny Willis, John Cowan and some of the other lads joined in in English. So we sang back and forth at each other for a bit, then someone shouted "Merry Christmas" and one of the Germans shouted "Fröhliche Weihnachten" then everyone was doing it, them and us.

There were a few shouts between officers on both sides and a truce was agreed – no firing so that each side could come out and collect the dead. But then we were all out in the open looking at each other, and they're just men, just like us. We talked, in sign language mostly, though some spoke English, and we swapped cigarettes and chocolate.

And then after a while we all climbed back down into our holes in the ground, and now we're watching each other wondering who'll start to fire again first and it all seems even more wrong. How can you shoot someone who gave you their chocolate?

CHRISTMAS GIFTS

Every Allied soldier received a present from Princess Mary, daughter of the British King George V. Princess Mary's Gift Fund boxes contained a Christmas card and photo of the princess, with a selection of presents including tobacco, cigarettes, chocolate and writing materials.

TUNNELLERS

Engineers and miners dug deep tunnels from their own lines to the enemy trenches, which were then filled with explosives to destroy the enemy's defences. It was a very dangerous job: tunnels collapsed on men as they worked. Both sides were digging, trying to intercept each other's tunnels, which led to underground battles.

3. INTO BATTLE

Did you know they fought battles in these stinky trenches for 4 years?

That's batty, Ratty!

I know, and neither side got anywhere until 1918!

That's totally batty, Ratty!

But over 12 million men were killed or injured.

That's mega batty, Ratty. What are people like?

BATTLE REPORT

MARNE, FRANCE

WHEN: September 1914 (4 days)
MISSION: Keep the Germans out of Paris.
CASUALTIES*: Allies 87,000, German 68,000
OUTCOME: The Allies defended Paris, but the Germans dug trenches and stayed in France for 4 years anyway.

* Dead, wounded and captured

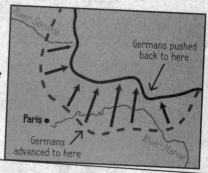

VERDUN, FRANCE

WHEN: February to December 1916 (10 months!)
MISSION: Stop the German advance.
CASUALTIES: Allies over 500,000, German over 400,000
OUTCOME: The French won the longest battle of the First World War and one of the bloodiest ever. But the Germans didn't surrender.

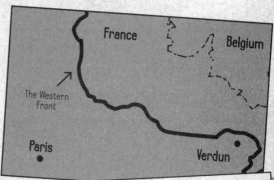

JUTLAND, THE NORTH SEA

WHEN: 31st May to 1st June 1916 (36 hours)
MISSION: Stop the German naval fleet.
CASUALTIES: Allies 14 ships, 6500 men. German 11 ships, 3000 men
OUTCOME: The only major sea battle in the First World War. Both sides claimed victory, but the German fleet never dared sail into the North Sea again during the war.

FLEURBAIX, FRANCE, 30TH JANUARY 1915

Under bombardment. Noise of shells terrifying. Very scared.
Many wounded.

FLEURBAIX, 8TH FEBRUARY 1915

Back in the reserve trenches. Supposed to be out of shell range
here. Shelling has stopped for a few hours, thank God. Well,
I've properly seen war now. It's almost impossible to describe.
The noise was incredible –
shells booming, the rat-tat-
tat of machine guns, the wasp
noise of bullets going past much
too close. Shouting, swearing,
orders, pleas, screams. Clods
of earth flying, bits of shrapnel,
lumps of barbed wire raining
down, broken bodies. I didn't
run away. I didn't wet myself.
I'm still here.

Lots of new weapons were developed during the First World War as both sides tried to outdo their enemy. They were often not tested properly and could be very unreliable.

Shrapnel shells exploded in the air, hurling out sharp metal fragments.

Grenades were thrown into enemy trenches. They had names like the 'Jam Tin' and 'Hairbrush' because of their shape.

Mortars were steel tubes used to fire large bombs.

High-explosive shells blew up when they hit trenches and buildings.

Machine guns were used to shoot advancing troops, firing 400-500 rounds of bullets per minute.

Poison gas, such as chlorine, phosgene and mustard gas, was used by both sides. Mustard gas burnt the skin, caused temporary blindness and damaged the lungs.

8th February 1915

Dear Mother and Father,

It's been a busy time in the trenches, but I'm away from the front line just now - a chance to catch up on sleep. It's been hard to get more than a couple of hours in the front trenches what with shelling, and the air a bit lively with bullets.

We've had some men killed and wounded, I'm afraid, but don't worry too much about me - I'm good at getting out of the way and small enough to shelter in holes that are too wee for anyone else!

Thank you for the socks. It's still very cold here, so it's wonderful to have warm, dry feet for a bit.

Your loving son, James

PASSED BY CENSOR
No 3743

FLEURBAIX, 17TH FEBRUARY 1915

Behind the lines for a few days rest with the lads. Been bicycling with Joe Cornwall, Jimmy Mogg and John Stewart. Felix bought me egg and chips in a café – best food I've had in weeks. Going back to the front line tomorrow, so I'll make the most of my last night in a bed for a bit.

WRITING HOME

Soldiers were allowed to write two letters home every week, which were read and censored to remove any military information or anything that might lower morale in Britain. If they were in a hurry, soldiers could fill in a Field Service postcard, crossing out the sentences they didn't need.

NOTHING is to be written on this side except the date and signature of the sender. Sentences not required may be erased. If anything else is added the post card will be destroyed.

[Postage must be prepaid on any letter or post card addressed to the sender of this card.]

I am quite well.

I have been admitted into hospital

{ sick } and am going on well.
{ wounded } and hope to be discharged soon.

I am being sent down to the base.

I have received your { letter dated _____
{ telegram " _____
{ parcel " _____

Letter follows at first opportunity.

I have received no letter from you
{ lately
{ for a long time.

Signature }
only }

Date _____

FESTUBERT, FRANCE, 20TH MAY 1915

We moved south a bit and we've been fighting for weeks now, but I don't know who's winning. Maybe no one. There are rumours that Jerry's using poison gas. We're supposed to be getting some sort of mask, but they haven't appeared yet. We're all exhausted, snatching sleep in funkholes when we can.

FESTUBERT, 22ND MAY 1915

Marched 20 miles through the night, now we're in position, front-line trenches. Don't recognise any landmarks. Where are we? Just mud and wire and bodies in front of us. Hard to work out what's going on, but things not going we—

FIRST-AID POST, BETHUNE, FRANCE
5TH JUNE 1915

I've had a lucky escape, though it didn't feel like it at the time. A shrapnel shell went off near me, blew me off my feet and half-buried me in earth. I've never been so frightened in my life. I was so busy scrabbling my way out of what felt like a grave that I didn't notice I'd been hit. Nothing serious, I know I was lucky. A couple of wee bits of shrapnel in my hand and a big graze on my side. Could have been much worse – whatever did it dinged off my bugle first. There's a big dent in it now. If I'd not gone back for it that time, maybe I'd be dead now.

Got the bandages off my hand yesterday, so now I can write – and fire my rifle – so I'm heading back into action again, just in time for my fifteenth birthday.

STEEL HELMETS

British troops didn't get steel helmets until 1916. Before that, they only had their uniform caps, which gave them no protection.

FACT-TASTIC FACT

LOOS, NORTHERN FRANCE, 10TH SEPTEMBER 1915

There have been so many night marches, moving north, I've lost count. Now we're in Loos and we're expecting to have a fight on our hands. Saw a dogfight between a German Fokker and one of our Bristol Scouts today. It was close enough for us to hear the bullets rattling off both planes. We cheered when we saw smoke coming from the Fokker's engine, then it spun round and round like a sycamore seed and fell and crashed in a great burst of flame. I know I should be pleased that it's one less German and one less German plane, but I can't help feeling sorry for the poor pilot.

AIRCRAFT

Aeroplanes were invented by the Wright Brothers in the USA in around 1903, only 11 years before war broke out. Early planes were used to spy behind enemy lines, but by 1915 planes with machine guns had 'dogfights' over battlefields. Later aircraft were able to drop bombs during battles, and to target enemy cities such as London. They went on to play a much bigger role in the Second World War.

SOPWITH CAMEL FIGHTER

NATION: Britain
CREW: 1
SPEED (km/h): 185
WINGSPAN (m): 8.53
WEAPONS: 2 machine guns
BOMBS: 4

GOTHA GV BOMBER

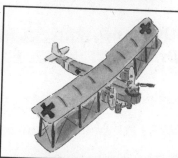

NATION: Germany
CREW: 3
SPEED (km/h): 140
WINGSPAN (m): 23.7
WEAPONS: 3 machine guns
BOMBS: 14

FOKKER DR1 TRIPLANE FIGHTER

NATION: Germany
CREW: 1
SPEED (km/h): 165
WINGSPAN (m): 7.2
WEAPONS: 2 machine guns
BOMBS: 0

HANDLEY PAGE BOMBER

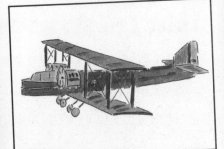

NATION: Britain
CREW: 3-6
SPEED (km/h): 157
WINGSPAN (m): 30.48
WEAPONS: 5 machine guns
BOMBS: 30

LOOS, 20TH SEPTEMBER 1915

We've moved right up to the front line now. No bombardment yet. Everyone seems to be waiting. We just keep digging new trenches and making the old ones deeper and putting out as much barbed wire as we can.

LOOS, 22ND SEPTEMBER 1915

Waiting's over. Big bombardment started yesterday. It's meant to destroy the German barbed wire so we can get through it easily, but I can still see a lot of intact wire from here.

LOOS, 25TH SEPTEMBER 1915

Worst day yet. The men who went over the top were just 100 yards from the enemy, then the German machine guns started up. Men were falling everywhere, like corn being scythed down. There were hundreds dead in less than a minute. We were screaming at them from our trenches.

"Take cover! Get down! Get in a shell hole!" But they didn't have time to do anything. Then the Germans suddenly stopped firing. Felix reckons even they were sickened by the slaughter. It's very quiet here now, no one's talking. We're all too shocked by what happened.

When we started firing we just had to load and reload. They went down in their hundreds. You didn't have to aim. We just fired into them.

German soldier's diary, Battle of Loos

WOUNDED SOLDIERS

All soldiers carried a 'field dressing' for basic first aid and there were first aid posts in the support trenches.

The Polish-French scientist Marie Curie, famous for her work on radioactivity, developed mobile X-ray vans during the First World War, helping to treat wounded soldiers on the Western Front.

"GO HOME AND SIT STILL!"

The Scottish doctor Elsie Inglis wanted to set up hospitals run by women doctors on the Western Front. She was a campaigner for women's rights and part of the suffragette movement. She ignored advice from the War Office to "go home and sit still" and raised money to set up the Scottish Women's Hospitals – but the British War Office didn't want them, so they worked with the other Allies instead. They ran hospitals in France, Greece and Serbia, where Elsie Inglis is still a famous hero.

Serious injuries were treated by nurses in Casualty Clearing Stations several kilometres behind the lines. Soldiers were patched up before being sent back to fight.

A 'Blighty' wound meant being sent back to Britain. Many men longed for a 'Blighty' - as long as it wasn't too serious.

Living in crowded, dirty trenches meant diseases like cholera, typhoid, measles and meningitis spread easily.

Many British women volunteered to be nurses. Some worked at home, others worked near the front line. The VADs (Volunteer Aid Detachments) didn't get paid at first and had to pay for their own uniforms!

4. THE HOME FRONT

LONDON, 1ST OCTOBER 1915

Home leave at last. Writing this as I wait for the train to Edinburgh. I try to imagine being able to sleep for a whole night, in a bed, with no chance I'll be blown to bits. It seems an impossible thing. I can't wait to get home, but I won't tell my family everything I've seen. Mother and Father would only worry about me even more.

DALKEITH, 3RD OCTOBER 1915

It's only now I know I'm safe that I realise how frightened I've been, day after day. I slept for 15 hours when I got home, and I've spent most of the time since I woke up eating – stovies, mince and tatties, fruit cake… I can't get enough. "You look as if you haven't had a proper meal since you went to France," Mother said, and set to feeding me up.

The first time she saw the scar on my side where the shrapnel grazed me, she didn't say anything at all, just put her hands over her mouth, then hugged me so tight I could hardly breathe. I know what she was thinking – I've thought it myself. "It's all right," I told her. "It's not as bad out there as you think."

My family can't imagine what it's really like in the trenches and I don't want them to. I try to make light of the danger and the cold and filth to Mother and Father, and to make it sound like an adventure to the wee ones. Agnes and Jenny told me all about the big map of the Front on the wall in their school. They move wee flags round to show what's happening, but they don't really understand, though some of their friends have had fathers or brothers killed. They're each knitting me a sock and they're having a competition to see who can finish first. I'm not sure they'll end up the same size, but at least they'll keep my feet warm.

William's managed to enlist in the Artillery, although he's only 17 and still underage, so I've been more honest with him.

I reckon he should know what he's getting into. "What's it like to kill a man?" he asked. He seemed disappointed when I said I hadn't killed anyone, haven't really been involved in the fighting yet, because I'm only 15. He doesn't understand. How could he? He's never seen men turned into lumps of meat.

DALKEITH, 5TH OCTOBER 1915

It's taken me a few days to realise how things have changed at home. The first thing I noticed was boys pulling hand carts, because so many horses have gone to the front, but the biggest change is how few men there are, and that means a lot more women are out working. My sister Margaret already had a job at the baker's, but Chrissie Green next door comes home yellow from handling explosives every night after working in the munitions factory at Roslin. That can't be good for you, and I've heard a few factories have gone up in flames.

CONKERS

During the war, British children collected conkers, which were processed to make a chemical that was used in explosives.

Chrissie's wee brother Geordie says his Scout troop's guarding the railway line and the reservoir. I thought I'd be able to go to the football while I was at home, but there are no matches now, because so many of the players are away.

WOMEN AT WORK

Before the war, women were treated as second-class citizens. Skilled jobs were seen as 'men's work' and most people thought 'a woman's place is in the home'. Women were expected to give up work if they married, and many women who did work were domestic servants. Women couldn't vote, but the suffragette movement was campaigning vigorously for this right.

With so many men away fighting, women took over jobs in shipyards, munitions factories and on farms; they drove buses and ambulances and delivered letters – some of them actually wore trousers! Some people thought they would be physically and morally harmed by war work, and might abandon their roles as mothers and home-makers. Of course, they were proved wrong.

> If the women in the factories stopped work for twenty minutes, the Allies would lose the war.

Field Marshall Joffre, British Army

A FIGHTING WOMAN

Yorkshire woman Flora Sandes went to Serbia as a nurse, but enrolled in the Serbian army once she was there. She was the only British woman who officially served as a soldier in the First World War.

A WOMAN ON THE FRONT LINE

Dorothy Lawrence wanted to be a war journalist, but no one would employ a woman for such a dangerous job. She disguised herself as a male soldier and went to the front line anyway, where she worked in the trenches for 10 days before handing herself over to the authorities.

FOOD SHORTAGES

By 1917 there were food shortages in Britain because so many supply ships were being sunk and in 1918 sugar, meat, flour, butter, margarine and milk were rationed. Even the King and Queen had ration cards. Food shortages were even worse in Germany. Bread was rationed from early 1915 and lentils and even sawdust were added to loaves.

MINISTRY OF FOOD.

NATIONAL RATION BOOK (B).

INSTRUCTIONS.

Read carefully these instructions and the leaflet which will be sent you with this Book.

1. The person named on the reference leaf as the holder of this ration book must write his name and address in the space below, and must write his name and address, and the serial number (printed upside down on the back cover), in the space provided to the left of each page of coupons.

Food Office of Issue: EDINBURGH   Date: MAR 16

Signature of Holder: Mrs R Marchbank

Address: 113 High Street Dalkeith

2. For convenience of writing at the Food Office the Reference Leaf has been put opposite the back cover, and has purposely been printed upside down. It should be carefully examined. If there is any mistake in the entries on the Reference Leaf, the Food Office should be asked to correct it.

3. The holder must register this book at once by getting his retailers for butcher's meat, bacon, butter and margarine, sugar and tea respectively, to write their names and the addresses of their shops in the proper space on the back of the cover. Persons staying in hotels, boarding houses, hostels, schools, and similar establishments should not register their books until they leave the establishment.

4. The ration book may be used only by or on behalf of the holder, to buy rationed food for him, or members of the same household, or guests sharing common meals. It may not be used to buy rationed food for any other persons.

[Continued on next page.]

N. 2 (Nov.)

IF FOUND, RETURN TO ANY FOOD OFFICE.

ROYAL FAMILY FIGHT

The British royal family has German ancestors – in fact, Kaiser Wilhelm, the German leader during the First World War, was Queen Victoria's grandson. During the war, the royal family changed their German surname 'Saxe-Coburg-and-Gotha' to 'Windsor'.

DALKEITH, 7TH OCTOBER 1915

I've caught up with what's been going on here. Went to the cinema to see a newsreel film today showing news from the war, and Father's been keeping bits of the papers for me.

5TH NOVEMBER 1914

GERMAN SPY TO BE EXECUTED

German Carl Lody will face death by firing squad tomorrow at dawn at the Tower of London. He is the first man to be executed there since 1741. Lody posed as an American tourist in Edinburgh to gather information about the Forth Rail Bridge and docks on the Firth of Forth, but his true intent was revealed when he sent his information abroad in un-coded messages.

8TH MAY 1915

LUSITANIA SUNK!

THE PASSENGER SHIP Lusitania left New York for Liverpool on 1st May carrying almost 2000 passengers. Disaster struck on 7th May, in waters south of Ireland, when a single torpedo from a German U-boat ripped the hull open. As the mighty ship wallowed, lifeboats crashed into the waves and passengers were thrown off their feet. Less than an hour later, the liner was on the seabed and 1198 souls, including over 120 Americans, had lost their lives.

BATTLE OF LOOS

GERMANS HEAVILY DEFEATED BY BRITISH

The Germans attacked our lines in great strength, but were beaten off and mown down by machine gun and artillery fire. The German dead are estimated between 7000 and 8000 – a complete and costly defeat for them. Our own casualties have proved to be even less than the original estimate and German claims of success have been exposed as blatant lies!

BRITONS! YOUR COUNTRY NEEDS YOU

KAISER BILL

TRADE MARK

KAISER'S FACE ON EVERY SHEET

KAISER'S FACE ON EVERY SHEET

TOILET PAPER

ALIENS!

Foreign nationals in Britain were known as 'aliens' and anyone the government thought may pose a threat to security was imprisoned.

FACT-TASTIC FACT

The papers make it sound as though we always win. I was at Loos and it wasn't like that at all. We lost far more men than the Germans did.

There are posters like this to make everyone at home keen to fight, but I know the Germans aren't really monsters. It's fun wiping your bum on the Kaiser's face though!

Father says it's harder than ever in the mines. A lot of the miners have gone to France as tunnellers and most of the pit ponies have been taken too. There's coal rationing at home now, so people have to be careful how much they use. We're lucky, though – Father manages to get us a wee bit extra because of his work.

HORSES

There weren't many motor vehicles yet, so horses were used to pull carts, ambulance wagons, field kitchens and artillery at the Front. The British Army probably used around 500,000 horses – and had to find food for them, which was a major problem.

I went up to the pigeon loft with Father this morning. He's got a couple of good young birds he'll start racing soon – he needs to have a licence for them now, to prove he's not a spy! They use them all the time in France: much more reliable for carrying messages than the field telephones – the cables are forever getting cut and then they're useless. And a pigeon's a smaller target for a sniper than a runner. I try not to think about that when I'm running with messages.

I start the long journey back to France tonight. I wonder what I'm going back to?

SPY PIGEONS

Belgian volunteers with baskets of pigeons were parachuted behind enemy lines to spy on German troops and send messages back to the Allies. But they weren't always keen to jump out of the plane, so planes were designed where the pilot pulled a lever, automatically dropping the man and his feathered friends.

ZEPPELIN RAIDS

Zeppelins were huge German airships used to patrol the North Sea and bomb towns in Britain and on mainland Europe.

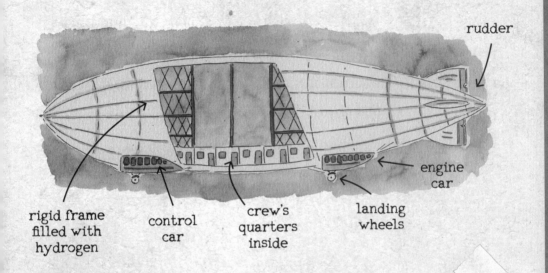

rudder

engine car

rigid frame filled with hydrogen

control car

crew's quarters inside

landing wheels

In April 1916, two zeppelins bombed Edinburgh, aiming for naval targets but hitting Leith and the city centre instead, and narrowly missing Edinburgh Castle. 13 people died, 24 were injured and several buildings were destroyed.

5. THE SOMME

THE SOMME, FRANCE, 20TH JUNE 1916

I'm back in France. A huge number of troops are moving up to the Front near the River Somme. There's a big push coming, but the commanders are trying to keep it secret from Jerry. I've been bringing up ammunition for the big guns and bullets by the thousand, carrying boxes forward from the reserve trenches. The trench system here is so big that the trenches have names to stop folk from getting lost, but you can't read the signs when it's dark. We're well back from the front line at the moment, but how long will that last?

THE SOMME, 28TH JUNE 1916

We're shelling the German trenches 24 hours a day, everyone's half-deaf from the constant racket. There's not been much coming back from them though. They must have taken shelter – or maybe they're dead already. We've been stuck fighting back and forth over the same few miles of ground

since the end of last year, but apparently there's a real chance of a big advance. "This could be the first step to ending this mess and getting home for Christmas," Felix said. My brother William's somewhere round here with a gun crew. Don't suppose he's getting much sleep – not that I am either. Even when you can hear that a shell won't hit you, you still feel the explosion in your guts and your teeth.

THE SOMME, 1ST JULY 1916

If I get out of this alive, I'll never forget what I've seen today. If hell really exists, it must be like this. The battle began this morning. When we blew the big mines near Lochnagar Road and Hawthorn Ridge the noise was so loud there's no way to describe it. I still can't hear properly. Our bombardment over the last few days was meant to destroy the German

BIG BANGS

At the time, the explosion of the Lochnagar mine was the loudest man-made sound in history, and was heard as far away as London. The crater it left is 91m across (the length of a football pitch) and 21m deep.

defences, but they must have been dug in much deeper than we thought. When our lads went over the top, the German machine guns and mortars started up and just kept on and on. There are so many men dead that it's like a carpet of bodies on the mud. And the wounded... We still can't get to them, even though it's dark now. We can hear them begging for help, but we daren't go out. I passed a man a while ago who was just curled up at the bottom of a trench, sobbing. I thought he was injured, but there wasn't a mark on him. "I want my mother. I have to go home," he kept saying. I didn't know what to do. I couldn't help him and I couldn't get him to move. In the end I had to leave him and go fetch the next lot of ammo I was meant to be delivering.

THE SOMME, 19TH JULY 1916

There are rumours that more than 19,000 men were killed just on the first day of the battle, and we're now 19 days in. Bodies are everywhere in no man's land. There's one leaning against what's left of a tree with a cigarette still in his mouth, even though he's dead. Train-loads of wounded leave all the time, there's no end to them.

The Germans have been using poison gas. We've got masks, but they're horrible to wear – everything's much harder to do when you can't see or hear properly. But I've seen men who've been gassed, so I don't waste any time putting mine on when the gas alarm sounds.

Last night I was taking rations to a communications trench and got lost. It was pitch black, no moon to help me. There was no one around, just me with my heart beating like a bird in a trap. Eventually I found some men and discovered I'd got into the front firing trench somehow. They showed me the way back and as I went I passed an artillery group. There was something familiar about one of the gunners, so I went a bit closer.

It was William!

We couldn't believe it – we were laughing and hugging each other like a right pair of loons, each so relieved to find the other alive.

We only had a few minutes together because we were both on duty, and I had to leave him. It's very hard to say goodbye when you know you might never see each other again.

YZEUX, FRANCE, 1st SEPTEMBER 1916

4 days in rest camp. First time in ages I've felt safe, though we can still hear the guns from here. What a luxury it is to get a decent sleep and a meal and clean clothes. I've even been riding a bicycle and swimming in the river. To think all these things felt normal once. Now they feel like part of a dream, and I'll wake up and be back in the mud and blood and terror and death and that'll feel more normal than this.

What has happened to the world?

THE IRON HARVEST

French and Belgian farmers still dig up about 900 tons of unexploded shells from the First World War every year when they are working their fields, about the weight of a large passenger aeroplane.

THE SOMME, 14TH OCTOBER 1916

Saw a tank today. A great, armour-plated thing, on caterpillar tracks, gun barrels poking out of the sides. It crushed everything in its way: wire, sandbags, trees, weapons, bodies. They're not fast, but they're terrifying. Thank God it's us that's got them, not Jerry. Even with the tanks, we're still fighting over the same bits of ground as we were back in July. Sometimes I think we'll be here forever. Maybe I'll die of old age if I don't get killed by a shell or a bullet.

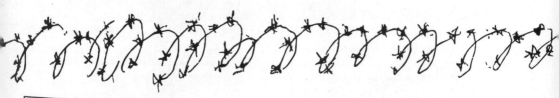

BATTLE REPORT: THE SOMME, FRANCE

WHEN: July to November 1916
MISSION: Break through German lines.
CASUALTIES: Allied 620,000, German 500,000.
OUTCOME: Battle ended due to flooding in November. The Allies moved forward just 8 miles.

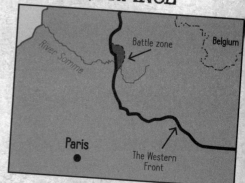

MARK I TANK

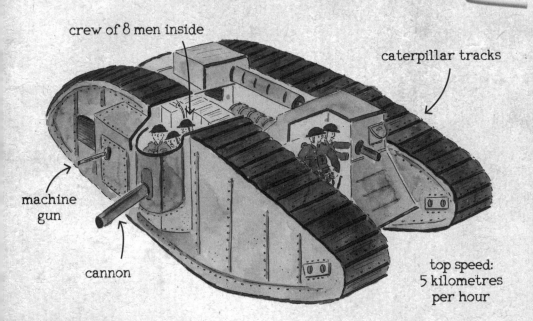

crew of 8 men inside

caterpillar tracks

machine gun

cannon

top speed: 5 kilometres per hour

Tanks were first used by the British during the Battle of the Somme, although most broke down before they reached German lines. Those that made it drove straight across narrow enemy trenches, clearing a path for soldiers to advance.

The official name for the first Mark I tank was His Majesty's Landship Centipede, but the troops called it Mother.

The Germans didn't have tanks until 1918.

THE WORLD AT WAR

During the First World War there was fighting almost EVERYWHERE.

Germany and Austria-Hungary were fighting Russia on the huge, cold Eastern Front.

Britain's friends in India, Australia and New Zealand helped the Allies too.

Britain and Germany both had colonies in Africa, so they fought there as well.

Italy was fighting Austria-Hungary high up in the snowy Alps.

Japan was fighting the German navy in the Far East.

The Ottoman Empire was fighting the Allies in Turkey and the Middle East.

LAWRENCE OF ARABIA

Captain T. E. Lawrence was a young British intelligence officer who fought with the Arab army against the Turks using guerrilla tactics such as night raids and destroying railway lines. His exploits inspired the famous film, *Lawrence of Arabia*.

6. THE WORLD AT WAR

POPERINGE, BELGIUM, 10TH JANUARY 1917

I've been here in Belgium since I came back from leave just
before Christmas. Things are quiet at the moment because of
the winter weather and I think both sides are still reeling from
those awful months on the Somme. I'm working as an officers'
servant now. I think Felix – Sergeant McNamara, I should call
him – arranged it somehow. "Fancy that!" he said when I
told him, and gave a big wink. I'm often in HQ, well behind
the lines – with much better food and quarters than usual.

There's a fair chance of keeping safe, dry, warm and fed, all at the same time, which feels too good to be true. And it's such a relief to be free of lice for a bit. Horrible things, much worse than rats. I sometimes cycle to the village for egg and chips – not as good as Mother's cooking, of course, but very tasty. I swim in the river, and I sometimes ride one of the ponies from the horse lines. I'm getting quite good at not falling off!

POPERINGE, 11th FEBRUARY 1917

Working for Captain Maude of the Intelligence Corps. He takes me out with him because he says my eyes and ears are sharper than his. Last night we crept into an old French trench and were close enough to the German front line to listen to their conversations. I didn't understand them, but the Captain speaks German, and he seemed pleased with whatever it was he had learned.

THE GOOD LIFE

Behind the lines, officers often stayed in large houses, with pianos, gramophones and much better food than the other soldiers. According to James's diary, the officers' menu for Christmas lunch 1917 at Piave Grappa was goose with apple sauce and cabbage, Christmas pudding and brandy sauce, whisky, port, wine and coffee – not that James got to eat all that!

FACT-TASTIC FACT

CODE TALKERS

After the USA joined the war their codes kept being broken, so they began to use Native American soldiers from the Choctaw tribe to pass messages in their own language over field telephones — completely baffling any Germans listening in. Written messages were often coded by jumbling up the letters and using a keyword. As each side worked out how to break the other's codes, more complex ones had to be developed.

Substitution codes use one letter to replace another. This can be made harder to crack by using a keyword. This is how it works:

Keyword (with no repeated letters)

SCOTLAND

Alphabet	A	B	C	D	E	F	G	H	I	J	K	L	M
Code	S	C	O	T	L	A	N	D	B	E	F	G	H

The letters of the keyword code for the first few letters

The remaining letters are entered in alphabetical order

N	O	P	Q	R	S	T	U	V	W	X	Y	Z
I	J	K	M	P	Q	R	U	V	W	X	Y	Z

Message: BOMBARDMENT TO BEGIN AT DAWN
Becomes: CJHCSPTHLIR RJ CLNBI SR TSWI

The letters are then arranged in groups of 5 to disguise words, giving:

CJHCS PTHLI RRJCL NBISR TSWIJ ←

> Extra 'nonsense' letter used to give final group of 5

It's very hard to decode the message without the keyword!

YOUR TURN TO DECODE!

Can you decode this message? The keyword is:

BAYONET

Message in CODE: XKSCB UNAPK GNJRC NYKON

Message in ALPHABET: ....

Alphabet	A	B	C	D	E	F	G	H	I	J	K	L	M
Code													

N	O	P	Q	R	S	T	U	V	W	X	Y	Z

POPERINGE, 7TH APRIL 1917

Yesterday the USA declared war on Germany at last.
Everyone here's very excited. When all the American troops
get here surely the German army won't be able to hold out
for long? That's what the officers are saying to each other,
anyway. I hope they're right!

Did you know the Americans didn't join the war until 1917?

Staying out of it was a good plan, if you ask me, Ratty.

But tricky when German U-boats torpedoed their ships.

True, Ratty, and then they intercepted a top-secret telegram from Germany encouraging Mexico to invade the USA.

Well, that really took the biscuit (mmm, biscuits...). They declared war on Germany and arrived in Europe in 1918.

Good job they did, Ratty, it changed everything...

GENOA, ITALY, 16TH NOVEMBER 1917

The Italian army's been in trouble since fighting started at Caporetto, high up in the Alps, so Britain and France are sending troops to help them – and I'm one of them. When you're down in a trench on the Western Front it's easy to forget the war's going on all over the world now.

We've had a great welcome. Played my bugle – first time for ages – as we marched to our quarters, folk cheering us on. People here are very relieved to have some help. It's freezing cold. We can see lots of snow on the mountains and we've been told that thousands of Italian troops have been killed by avalanches.

FREEDOM FOOD

During the First World War, some foods with German names were renamed in the USA. Hamburgers became 'Salisbury steak', Frankfurters turned into 'Liberty sausages'. Even Dachshund dogs were renamed and became 'Liberty dogs'!

PIAVE GRAPPA, ITALY, 26TH DECEMBER 1917

Huge attack on the aerodrome here this morning. Counted 43 enemy aircraft. Never seen anything like it – amazing! British, French and Italian planes after them. We could hear their machine guns even down here as we watched the dogfights, and heard the ack-ack of the anti-aircraft guns from the airfield. At least 12 German planes downed, 7 by anti-aircraft fire, 5 by our aircraft. I saw 4 of them go down,

a great whoosh of flame as they each hit the ground. Last few days here, then back to France for me, and a month in training camp. Can't believe I have to go back to training. I've been a soldier for nearly three years – if I didn't already know what I was doing, I'd be dead by now!

ARRAS, FRANCE, 4TH FEBRUARY 1918

Passed all my retraining tests and back with the Battalion at last. Felix – Sergeant McNamara – was there to meet me when I arrived. It's been months since I've seen everyone, not that they're all still alive. James Vickers and John Stewart were both killed last month. I've almost got used to people I know being killed. It shouldn't be like that.

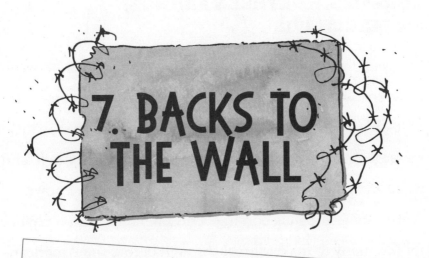

7. BACKS TO THE WALL

17TH DECEMBER 1917

GERMANY AND RUSSIA DECLARE PEACE

IT IS REPORTED that an armistice has been signed between Germany and the new government of the Russian Republic. Russia will play no further part in the war, releasing hundreds of thousands of German troops from fighting on the Eastern Front. It is inevitable that their attention will soon be turned towards the Western Front instead.

DOIGNIES, NORTHERN FRANCE, 8TH MARCH 1918

I've been made a battalion runner, taking messages between the trenches and battalion HQ. Felix wanted to get me out of it – it's a dangerous job, runners get targeted to stop the messages getting through. I've got to do my bit, though, and we're all in danger, so I told him not to. Everyone knows there's something big coming. This might be the last chance for Germany to make a breakthrough before the Americans get here in strength. It looks bad for us. With Russia out of the war the Germans have got almost a million extra troops to use here.

DOIGNIES, 22ND MARCH 1918

It's begun. Huge barrage and gas attack at 3 am. Bad casualties, more broken-hearted families. Trying to dig trenches under shell fire this morning, hiding in shell holes.

We're being forced back all the time. Ground that took months to gain and we've lost it in a few days. Aeroplane and machine-gun attacks as well as shells. Enemy attack at dusk, but our tanks pushed them back, thank God. Trying to snatch some sleep in a trench now.

VILLE CHAPELLE, 11TH APRIL 1918

More ground lost. We've had an order from the top commander, General Haig: "Every position must be held to the last man... With our backs to the wall... each one of us must fight to the end." He means we're all likely going to die and we have to fight until it happens. Running with messages again. Must have gone miles. Dodging bullets and shells all the time. So tired that I can't make sense of anything. More casualties: Tommy Turnbull, Lieutenant Dods, Jimmy Mogg. Soon there'll be no one left, nothing but empty uniforms in empty trenches, empty beds at home.

PARADIS, 13TH APRIL 1918

Battalion HQ captured. Many men taken prisoner, only about 50 of our battalion alive and uncaptured out of 600. Can't believe I'm still alive. Given orders to deliver a message to the first HQ I could find. Bullets all round me when I was running over the canal bridge, couldn't find anyone to deliver the message to. HQ just a pile of rubble and bodies. Running along the canal bank when a shell exploded so close it knocked me out. No idea how long I lay there. It was pitch dark when I came round –

thought I was dead at first – then I heard English voices. Don't mind admitting I wept with relief. Followed the sounds until I reached the road and found them, and an officer pointed me to temporary HQ in this farmhouse. They gave me some food – first in four days. Woke up face down in it hours later – still ate every last bit.

PARADIS, 14TH APRIL 1918

More deaths among our men today. Worst of all is Felix McNamara. He was killed on the IIth, but I only found out today. He tried so hard to keep me safe, but in the end he couldn't do the same for himself. Don't know how much more of this I can bear. I keep remembering that soldier I found sobbing in the trench during the Battle of the Somme. Is someone going to find me like that soon?

ST HILAIRE, 17TH APRIL 1918

Out of the battle line, thank God. I've been promoted to
Lance Corporal, so I'll get a pay rise – and I've been awarded
the Military Medal for Bravery in the Field for delivering
that message on the 13th. I'm just glad to be alive after what
happened that day. Hardly anyone is left now.

VIMY RIDGE, 17TH MAY 1918

Thousands of Americans have arrived over the last few days. Surely this will swing things for us? They're all well fed and healthy and smart – make us look like scarecrows. They're a friendly lot, keen to hear what we've been through. "Kid, tell us what it's been like. How do you keep warm in a trench in the winter? What are the French like to fight alongside?" They're generous too, giving us chocolate and cigarettes, but we'd be glad to see them whatever they were like. I met one who's just a few months older than me – another fool like William who lied his way into the army underage – called Frank McIntosh, whose grandparents emigrated to the USA from Dundee. He wanted to know all about Scotland – makes a nice change from being asked about the fighting.

NAMING THE WAR

At the time, the war was known as 'The Great War' or – optimistically – 'The War to End All Wars'.

BATTLE REPORT: THE SPRING OFFENSIVE, FRANCE

WHEN: April to July 1918

MISSION: Destroy the Allies and take Paris.

CASUALTIES: Allied 856,000, German 688,000

OUTCOME: The Germans attacked strongly along the Western Front with the extra troops released from the Eastern Front, but they ran out of supplies and their soldiers were exhausted. The Allies began to drive the German army back, and once American troops arrived, the Germans were pushed back even faster.

REIMS, 20TH JULY 1918

We've moved a long way south. Fierce fighting again. The Germans have had their backs to the wall since the Yanks arrived, so they're throwing everything they've got left at us. Many casualties. Will there be anyone left to go home when this ends? They say the end is close now, but it doesn't feel like it on a day like this.

REIMS , 27TH JULY 1918

The Germans have gone, from here at least! Blessed silence. No shells, no bullets, no wounded men screaming. We're all trying not to get our hopes up, but it's hard.

ARRAS, 19TH AUGUST 1918

Haven't been involved in any fighting since July 26th, although it's still going on near here. Perhaps I'm safe at last. Perhaps I dare start thinking about going home. Haven't heard from William since middle of July, but I've been on the move so much, a letter could easily be chasing me round France. That's what I tell myself anyway.

ARRAS, 25TH AUGUST 1918

I was a fool to think I was safe. I've taken a hit from mustard gas. I didn't even realise it had happened until I started coughing hours later. I've survived so much and now this. Can't see properly to write.

BATTLE REPORT:
THE HUNDRED DAYS OFFENSIVE, FRANCE

WHEN: August to November 1918
MISSION: Drive the Germans out of France.
CASUALTIES: Between 1,500,000 and 2,250,000 in total, but no one really knows.
OUTCOME: With American help, the Allies win.

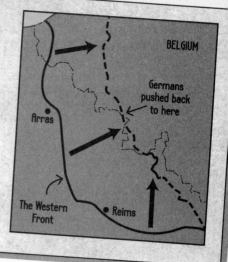

CAMIERS HOSPITAL, NORTHERN FRANCE, 29TH AUGUST 1918

One of the other chaps is writing for me. Still can't see properly. Hurts to breathe. Marked 'Blighty', now waiting to be evacuated. My war is over, but I'm more frightened than ever. Don't know how badly the gas has got me. Only good news is that William is safe. Nurse read me his letter yesterday.

Dear James,

It looks as though it's nearly over. I've been moving around as the front line goes back and forth, but it's all forward now. I'm off the line and in rest camp at Boulogne. Thought I might run into you after what happened on the Somme! I pray every night that you're safe and that we'll see each other at home very soon.

William

BARNET WAR HOSPITAL, ENGLAND, 11TH NOVEMBER 1918

The Armistice was signed at 11 o'clock this morning. The war is over at last. Really over. We can hear folk singing and dancing outside in the streets of London, but those of us here are still too crocked to join in much. Most of us have cried with relief, but we feel terrible, remembering all the men we knew who'll never come home again, all the parents and sweethearts who have lost their boys, all the children who have lost their fathers. We must never let anything like this happen again.

DALKEITH, SCOTLAND, 24TH DECEMBER 1918

Arrived a few hours ago, to find William already here. I don't think he and Mother believed I'd got over being gassed until they saw me. There were tears all round, a mixture of happy and sad. It's my first Christmas here since 1913 when I was 13 years old. Now I'm 18, still too young to be sent abroad if I enlisted today. Everything seems strange, as though it's not real. I've got so used to home being in my dreams, I suppose it'll take a while to believe in it again.

There's a photo on the mantelpiece of me playing the drum that was taken a few days before I left for France. I'm just a wee laddie. What were they thinking of, sending me to war? I'd no idea what would happen, thank God. The carefree wee lad in the photo never came home, of course.

ARMISTICE

After the war, many of the big empires that had ruled Europe were broken up, and some countries became independent for the first time.

9TH NOVEMBER 1918
Kaiser Wilhelm, the German ruler, abdicated and no longer ruled Germany.

11TH NOVEMBER 1918
British, French and German leaders met in a railway carriage in France and signed the Armistice at 11 am. The guns fell silent and the fighting stopped. Church bells were rung all over Europe.

4TH JANUARY 1919
The leaders of Britain, the USA and France met at a peace conference in Paris.

28TH JUNE 1919
The Treaty of Versailles was signed by 32 countries, officially ending the war, exactly 5 years after the assassination of Franz Ferdinand triggered it. Germany was forced to pay billions of pounds to the countries affected.

WOMEN'S RIGHTS

When men came back from the war, many women were expected to return to being wives and mothers, but their war experiences had given them confidence to work outside the home. In 1918, middle and upper class women aged over 30 were allowed to vote. It was just the start of the journey towards equality for women.

THE LEAGUE OF NATIONS

This organisation was formed by the 32 countries who signed the Treaty of Versailles, aiming to protect world peace. It failed in the 1930s, when the unthinkable happened again – the Second World War.

SHELL SHOCK

The terrors of being under shell fire and watching men die caused some soldiers to suffer from shell shock, which we now call post-traumatic stress disorder (PTSD). They could become paralysed, mute, blind or deaf. Some of them tried to walk away from the trenches, and were shot for desertion or cowardice.

SPANISH FLU

The death toll didn't slow down with the end of the war. Over the next 18 months Spanish flu affected almost every country in the world and killed over 50 million people - some scientists think as many as 100 million. In a horrible twist, it was most likely to kill young people, many of them the soldiers who had survived the war.

THANKFUL VILLAGES

There are 53 villages in England and Wales in which all the men who went to fight survived. There are no Thankful Villages in Scotland or Ireland.

8. REMEMBRANCE

DALKEITH, 11TH NOVEMBER 1921

Today was the dedication of the new War Memorial. A great crowd came to pay their respects. It's so hard to read all those names and know they're gone. I'll not write them here, they're written in stone now. I don't need to anyway – they still go round and round in my head, Felix most of all. I was asked to play the Last Post at the ceremony. First time I've played my bugle since I came back. I was afraid I wouldn't get through it, but I did, though the crowd around me couldn't hold back their tears. I managed to save mine for later, when I was alone.

This is the last entry I'll make in this diary. When I read it now, I can't believe how the world has changed. Jobs are harder to come by even though so many men are gone. The maps I grew up with have all been redrawn – countries have appeared and disappeared. I've changed too. I thought we were off on an adventure and we'd all be home again soon. I didn't understand anything when I left for France.

It's just as well. No one would have gone if they could have seen the future. But I know I'm one of the lucky ones, and I'm going to make the most of my life now.

REMEMBRANCE

WAR MEMORIALS

Almost every town and village in Britain has a war memorial to commemorate those who died during the First World War and later conflicts. In France and Belgium, thousands of soldiers are buried in huge cemeteries, but many bodies were never recovered and still lie under the old battlefields. Services of remembrance take place every year on 11th November, the day the Armistice was signed.

WAR POETS

Many poets wrote about their experiences in the trenches. Among the most famous are Wilfred Owen and Siegfried Sassoon, who met in Edinburgh in 1917, when they were both being treated in Craiglockhart Hospital for shell shock. Owen was killed on the Western Front on 4th November 1918. His mother received the news as the church bells were ringing in celebration on Armistice Day.

POPPIES

Many people wear poppies as a sign of remembrance,
because they grow on the battlefields of the
Western Front. John McCrae, a Canadian soldier,
wrote this famous poem:

In Flanders fields the poppies blow
Between the crosses, row on row,
That mark our place; and in the sky
The larks, still bravely singing, fly
Scarce heard amid the guns below.

We are the Dead. Short days ago
We lived, felt dawn, saw sunset glow,
Loved and were loved, and now we lie,
In Flanders fields.

Take up our quarrel with the foe:
To you from failing hands we throw
The torch; be yours to hold it high.
If ye break faith with us who die
We shall not sleep, though poppies grow
In Flanders fields.

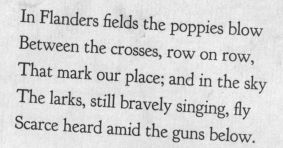

9. THE REAL JAMES MARCHBANK

The diary entries in this book are closely based on the diary of James Marchbank, who was born in Edinburgh in June 1900 and was brought up in Dalkeith. He had six siblings including his brother, William. Shortly before he left school in 1914, he joined the 1/8th Royal Scots Territorial Battalion as a drummer and bugler.

Although he was only 14 when war broke out, he served on the Western Front for most of the war. He recorded many of his experiences in a diary, which was actually forbidden in case it fell into enemy hands. He really did bump into his brother at the Battle of the Somme. Quite something, since 390,000 British troops were involved.

Both brothers survived the war, but in April 1917, while they were fighting on the Western Front, their father was killed in a mining accident, back in Dalkeith.

The real James Marchbank, 1915

From left: James, Margaret, William, Jenny and Agnes, 1908

14

Nov 11ᵈ 1914 WILL.

In the event of my death I give the whole of my property and effects to my Mother

Mrs. R. Marchbank
113. High Street
Dalkeith
Midlothian
Scotland

Bugler J. Marchbank.
8ᵗʰ Royal Scots

Nov 11ᵗʰ 1914.

Their mother was left to bring up their younger siblings alone and with very little money.

After the war, James worked as a railwayman, married and had a family of his own. He died in 1976. His family remembers him as a quiet and modest man, who never talked about his war experiences, although his grandchildren do remember him playing the bugle to wake them when they stayed with him. James' family still treasure his medals, diary – and his bugle.

James, around 1916

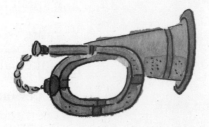

Gill Arbuthnott is the author of many non-fiction books and novels for children, including Chaos Clock, Chaos Quest, Winterbringers and Dark Spell. She lives in Edinburgh with her family and Leonard the cat.

Darren Gate is an illustrator and graphic designer based in Scotland. He won the Kelpies Design & Illustration Prize in 2016. He currently lives in Glasgow with his partner and 3 loud budgies.

ACKNOWLEDGEMENTS

I couldn't have written this book without masses of help. Thanks to Tony Cook, Col Robert Watson, Tom Gordon, Helen Spence, John Duncan and the staff of Dalkeith Museum for introducing me to James. Alan Cummings told me all about Elsie Inglis and Linda Brooks about homing pigeons. Sarah Heintze and George Harris kindly checked the manuscript for historical howlers – any that remain are my fault!

The biggest thankyou, however, goes to James Marchbank's son Robert, niece Margaret and grandchildren Gillian, Lesley and, especially, Neil for their generosity in sharing their memories of James and allowing me to use his story here. I hope he would approve of the result.

– Gill Arbuthnott

BONUS FACT-TASTIC FACTS!

SPIES

Both sides used spies. The most famous was probably a woman known as Mata Hari, who worked as a dancer and a double agent, spying for both France and Germany. She was caught and shot in France in 1917.

FLAMING BAYONETS

Flaming bayonets were invented in America. Containers of fuel were attached to the end of rifles, and when lit they produced huge flames. Thankfully they were never used in battle.

CHILDREN AT WAR

Schools in Britain raised money to help the war effort. Newbattle School near Edinburgh raised the fabulous sum of £5000 and was among the top five fundraising schools in the UK.

Scouts guarded railways and reservoirs and kept a lookout for zeppelin raids, Guides prepared hostels and first-aid stations and helped in government offices, and Sea Scouts kept watch around the coast for invasion. In the cities, children collected scrap metal, and in the countryside, sphagnum moss, which was used to dress wounds.

TAKING SIDES

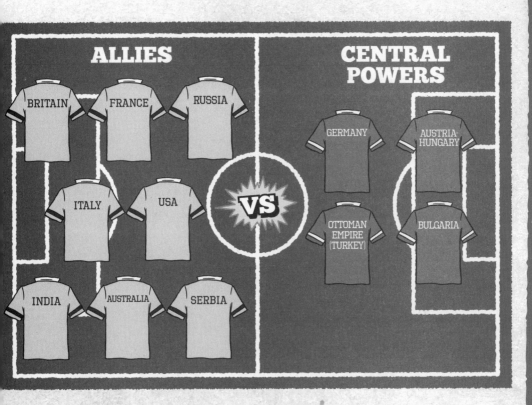

ALLIES

BRITAIN FRANCE RUSSIA

ITALY USA

VS

INDIA AUSTRALIA SERBIA

CENTRAL POWERS

GERMANY AUSTRIA-HUNGARY

OTTOMAN EMPIRE (TURKEY) BULGARIA

In total, around 50 countries were involved in the First World War.

PROPAGANDA

The governments of both Britain and Germany spread lies about the enemy to encourage their soldiers to keep fighting. It was rumoured in Britain that the Germans had a special factory where they turned the bodies of dead soldiers into explosives (not true).

BOOM!

In 1955 lightning set off an unexploded mine from the First World War under a Belgian farm, killing a cow. There is at least one more huge unexploded mine still down there.

MEDALS

James Marchbank was awarded the Military Medal for 'acts of gallantry and devotion to duty under fire'. The Victoria Cross (VC), the highest award British servicemen can receive, is awarded for 'conspicuous bravery... in the presence of the enemy'.

ANIMALS REMEMBERED

There is an 'Animals in War' memorial in London and the inscription on it reads:

> *This monument is dedicated to all the animals*
> *that served and died alongside British and Allied*
> *forces in wars and campaigns throughout time.*
> *They had no choice.*